An Alaskan Adventure with Archer & Ember

Follow Archer & Ember's real life adventures on Facebook and Instagram
@red_husky_adventures

It's a beautiful winter day in Alaska.
Ember and Archer are two red Huskies outside playing,
Archer is happy chasing his ball
but Ember is on the trail of something else

Sniff...

A snow bunny runs out from under a tree,
Ember takes off after it!

Archer notices his sister chasing a bunny
and takes off after it too!

Bunnies are fast,
but huskies are too!

Splash! Through a river

Up a hill

down a hill

Through a field of tall grass

around a twisty tree

they are right on his tail-
    then POP!
The bunny disppears into a hole in the ground.

"Hmm..." Ember pokes her nose into the hole.
Archer looks around and notices it's getting dark.
"I don't know where we are" he says to Ember.

Ember looks around and says, "Oh no..."
Archer frowns and says, "I'm hungry! We are going
to miss dinner!"

"Shh" Ember says, "you're always hungry."
Feeling lost Ember looks left,
then right.

Suddenly there's a swift wind over the pups and they look up.

"I only see the moon" Archer says
"Climb to the nearest mountain and you will see"
the raven caws and disappears.

Ember and Archer look up, but only see the moon.
"Let's get a closer look" Ember says to Archer.
They climb to the top of the nearest hill

They look left, they look right.
Nothing.
They keep walking.

The pups walk up on a herd of caribou.
"We are lost" Archer says to a caribou.

"Let the lights guide you" the caribou says.
"I don't see the lights, I only see stars" Ember replies.
"Look north" says another caribou.

Ember and Archer look north,
    they can see a very dim color of light in the sky.
        "There!" Archer yells and the pups take off towards the light.

They are running so fast,
excited to get home when Archer trips over a rock!
"Ouch!" the rock cries.

But it's not a rock, it's a bear cub!
Momma bear isn't far behind
and she isn't happy her cub is hurt,
she takes off after Ember and Archer.

"Run!" Ember yells.

Huskies are one of the fastest breeds of dogs,
they are made to run fast for long distances.
They soon lose angry momma bear.
"That was close!" Archer yells to Ember.

They look up, the lights in the sky
are dancing with color.
Green, pink, yellow...
the pups chase the lights as fast as they can.

They run around the twisty tree

through a field of tall grass

Up a hill

down a hill

Splash! Through a river

"We're almost there!" Archer yells.

The pups can see home
in the distance.
"Hooray!" Ember yells.
"I can't wait to have dinner!"
says Archer.

Just then,
a snow bunny
hops out in front of Ember.

She looks towards home,
then back at the snow bunny
hopping away into the woods.

...Sniff

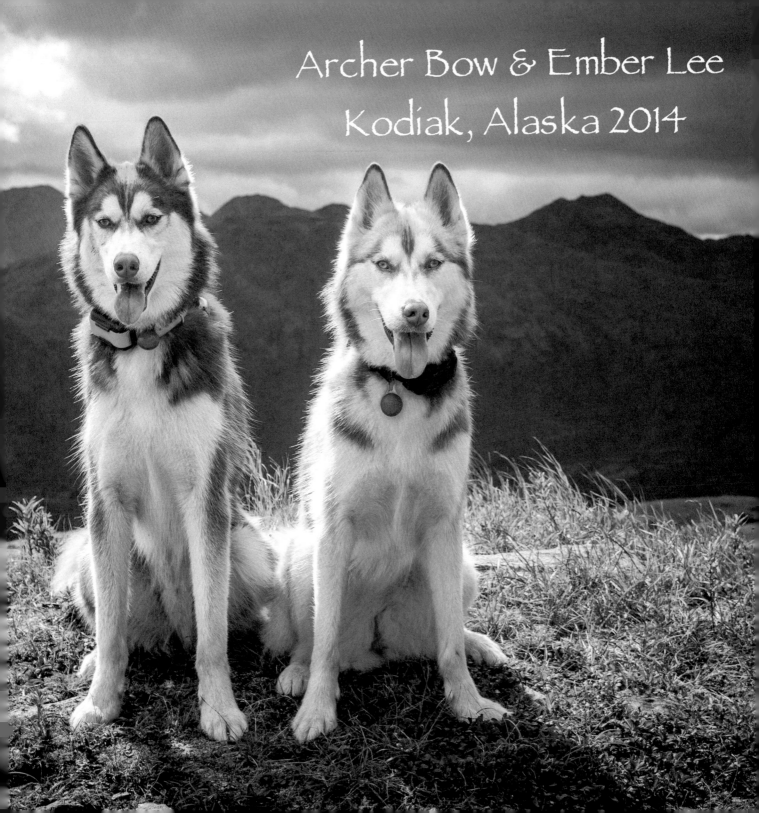

Archer Bow & Ember Lee
Kodiak, Alaska 2014

To my little loves, they bring such wonderful joy,
laughter and love into my life every single day;
for it is their unconditional love that inspired this book.
For my amazing husband, thank you for supporting my
dream. To my partner in crime- Annjannette, thank you
for not only making my dream come true but also for
becoming a dear friend.
-Krystin

For Anja, my little adventure
and for Shawn, for the big adventures.
-Annjannette

Made in the USA
San Bernardino, CA
06 December 2017